Bonnie Prince Charlie

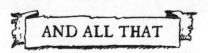

AND ALL THAT

Bonnie Prince Charlie

AND ALL THAT

Allan Burnett

Illustrated by Scoular Anderson

BIRLINN

First published in 2006 by
Birlinn Limited
West Newington House
10 Newington Road
Edinburgh
EH9 1QS

www.birlinn.co.uk

Reprinted 2011

ISBN 13: 978 1 84158 496 6

British Library Cataloguing-in-Publication Data
A catalogue record for this book is available from the British Library

Designed by James Hutcheson
Typeset by Iolaire Typesetting, Newtonmore
Printed and bound by Cox & Wyman Ltd, Reading

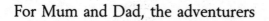
For Mum and Dad, the adventurers

Contents

Prologue

Bonnie Prince Charlie hid in the heather with his pistol drawn. He could hear the voices of enemy redcoat soldiers chatting to each other nearby. Luckily, they hadn't seen him yet. But one wrong move and Charlie knew he'd be dead.

Just a few months before, Charlie had marched through the British Isles with an army of loyal warriors at his side, conquering all who stood in his path. But now he was on the run in the Highlands of Scotland as a fugitive – a wanted man.

So how did Charlie plan on getting himself out of this mess? And how did things go so wrong in the first place?

Well, let's start at the beginning. You see, Charlie was born to get into trouble . . .

1

Born to be king

Fireworks shot into the night sky above the city of Rome, showering sparks of colour over the streets below, where people danced in celebration. They had just heard the news that in the Palazzo Muti, one of Rome's royal houses, a prince had been born.

He was a very special prince. So special that a thunderous salute was fired by the cannons of the ancient Saint Angelo Castle, on the banks of Rome's River Tiber, to honour his birth. The date was 31 December 1720 – New Year's Eve. And the arrival of this royal newcomer gave people an extra reason to celebrate the beginning of the new year.

So what was so special about this little baby prince? Perhaps it was the length of his name: Charles Edward Louis John . . . (wait for it) . . . Casimir Silvester Xavier . . . (phew) . . . Maria . . . (okay, I'm getting tired now) . . . Stuart.

I christen this baby Charles, Edward, John ...sorry...Louis... er... John, Silimir... oops... Casimir... Silver... I mean... Silvester...X...er... something ... Maria ... Maria?.... oh, let's just call him Charlie!

The prince's name was so long that it almost felt like New Year had come around again by the time people got to the end of saying it! But his name wasn't what made him special. Thankfully, the prince soon had a nickname that was a lot shorter anyway – Bonnie Prince Charlie.

Charlie was called 'bonnie' because he was a very handsome and pretty child. But that isn't the reason why he was special, either.

To find out why Charlie was special we have to leave Rome for a moment and look away over at the kingdom of Scotland, where people had just finished celebrating the New Year when they heard about Charlie's birth.

The news made the Scots celebrate all over again. Why? Because although Charlie had been born in Rome, he was actually a Scottish prince. In fact, Charlie was the latest in a long line of Scottish kings and queens called the Stuarts.

Lately, things had gone very badly for the Stuarts. Once upon a time they had ruled over the three kingdoms of the British Isles – Scotland, Ireland, and England and Wales (Wales was ruled by the kingdom of England).

About thirty years before Charlie was born, the Stuarts became very unpopular and had all their crowns taken away from them. They were told to get lost . . . and so they ended up in Rome.

But a lot of people in Scotland and across the British Isles now realised a terrible mistake had been made – and they wanted the Stuarts to come back! They hoped Charlie would be up to the job of helping to win back his family's crowns and one day become king himself.

And THAT is why Charlie was so special.

In fact, it even seemed like Charlie had come into the world with special, magical powers. The night he was born, a new star appeared in the sky. People thought the star was a sign that Charlie's quest to win back his family's kingdoms was sure to succeed . . .

2

Little action man

Charlie certainly got off to a flying start in life. He was full of beans and grew up crawling, running and jumping all over his parents' Roman palace. He had dark red hair, brown eyes and fair skin. (In portraits it looks like Charlie had white hair, but that was actually a powdered white wig, which was the fashion in those days.)

When Charlie's family weren't in Rome they spent time in the nearby city of Bologna. Perhaps Charlie liked eating spaghetti Bolognese for dinner?

As it happens, if Charlie did or didn't like something, he could be very stubborn about it. He was a headstrong little fellow. For instance, when Charlie was three, he caused quite a stir when his parents took him to meet the most powerful man in Rome – Pope Benedict XIII.

Now, it was a tradition that when you met the pope you had to kiss his feet. Charlie's mum and dad did it, so the little prince was expected to do the same. But Charlie refused! Who knows, perhaps the pope had really smelly feet?

Anyway, this showed that Charlie was afraid of nobody – not even a very powerful man like the pope. And he wasn't afraid of taking on new challenges, either. By the time Charlie was six and a half, he had learned lots of skills:

1. He could read a book.
2. He could ride a horse.
3. He could fire a gun.

Charlie could also use a crossbow and, according to one report, fire it from the street and hit birds perched up on the roof. Apparently, you could throw a ball in the air and Charlie would guarantee to split it in two with a single arrow.

Charlie could also speak many languages, including Italian, French, English and Latin. Knowing such languages was very important for any young prince who wanted to win friends and influence people.

Unfortunately, learning languages also meant Charlie understood everything his parents said to each other – most of which wasn't very nice. Charlie's mum and dad were both pretty weird, which was bad enough. But worse, they absolutely hated each other's guts.

Growing up when your parents do nothing but argue is horrible and must have made Charlie very sad. His mum was a young woman from Poland called Maria Clementina Sobieska and she was about half the age of Charlie's dad. When the couple got married, Charlie's dad was thirty but his mum was only sixteen – and they hardly knew each other.

It didn't take many years before Charlie's mum got fed up. She even went away and left her family for a year to live with nuns in a convent.

Meanwhile, Charlie was left at home with his dad and a brother, Henry, who was born in 1725. Charlie soon noticed that his dad preferred Henry to him, because Henry was better than Charlie at things like reading books and speaking different languages.

The feeling that you are not the favourite, that you are just second best, is not a very nice one. It seems to have made Charlie very competitive and eager to impress

9

others. And what with all his parents' arguments, and the fact his mum just gave up and left home for a long time, life must have seemed to Charlie like one long battle.

Charlie grew determined that he would try to win all the battles and struggles that life threw at him. So he became a little action man. Whenever he got the chance, he threw aside his homework and headed outdoors. With his horses and guns, he became a keen hunter. He also liked playing golf, tennis and badminton.

The more Charlie fought to win at sports and games, or hunted with guns, the more he realised his dream was to fight real, military battles. He wanted to lead an army.

So, to make himself tough like a proper soldier, Charlie went on long walks without any shoes on. He also read military manuals that taught you how to beat your enemies.

And he studied plans of fortifications – like walls, fences, gates and ditches – and built his own model forts and castles.

But before long, Charlie grew tired of models and toy soldiers. He wanted some real action . . .

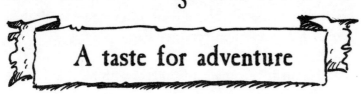

3

A taste for adventure

Charlie got his first taste of a real battle when he was just thirteen. It was 1734 and an Italian city called Gaeta was under siege. Charlie was invited to go and watch the siege army trying to capture it.

This was very dangerous because Charlie had to crouch alongside the invading soldiers in the trenches they had dug around the city. The teenage prince was right in the firing line and might have been killed.

Luckily, some people with very special powers were watching over Charlie from afar to try to make sure no harm came to him. For example, the new pope, Clement XII, got on very well with the young prince. (Clement must have had nice, clean feet!) He had given Charlie money so that he would be well cared for on his military adventure.

Meanwhile, Charlie's mum told her new friends – all the nuns in Rome – that they must pray to God to keep her son safe.

It seemed to do the trick. Charlie kept cool in the trenches and didn't get himself killed. He also got on well with the soldiers, who were a mixture of Spaniards, Italians and Walloons. (The Walloons came from a place that is now part of Belgium.) Using his language skills, Charlie cracked jokes for the men in their own tongues to lift their spirits. This made him very popular:

1. He made the Spaniards snigger with his sidesplitting Spanish silliness.
2. He made the Italians' eyes water with his incredible Italian impersonations.
3. And he made the Walloons wince by warbling at them in Walloon. (Walloon was a funny kind of French.)

Charlie's jokes worked a treat. The invading army was successful and the city was captured. The prince's ability to get on with common folk, instead of just being a snobby royal, was a real talent. It would stand him in good stead later on.

A year after Charlie made his first mark on the battlefield, his mum became very ill after she stopped eating properly and became worn out. In January 1735, she died. Poor Charlie was still only fourteen.

To try to take his mind off this horribly sad event, Charlie played the cello. But it was only when he went travelling that he really began to perk up.

Charlie went on a tour all around Italy and was invited to lots of parties and banquets. He was very popular – especially with girls, who found him kind, charming and very handsome. His moves on the dance-floor made them go weak at the knees.

But Charlie wasn't really a big fan of parties. He preferred to be out training hard to improve his military skills and teaching his body to endure hardship.

But why would Charlie give himself such a hard time when he could just take it easy, feast at every banquet in Italy and charm all the ladies? Well, he had more important things on his mind. At one party, he turned to somebody else and said, 'Had I soldiers, I would not be here now.'

So where would he be?

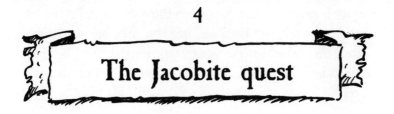

4

The Jacobite quest

If Charlie had soldiers, he would be in Britain. In fact, he constantly dreamed of taking an army to the British Isles to win back his family's kingdoms.

Many times as a young lad, Charlie had listened to the story of his Stuart ancestors and how they lost their thrones. It was a tale about doing your duty, of having loyalty and courage. But it was also a tale of selfishness, arrogance and cowardice.

The story taught Charlie the importance of doing the right thing and knowing when to do it. And, more importantly, of not doing the wrong thing and knowing when not to do it!

Most importantly, it taught Charlie that a king should be reasonable and listen to his subjects – or he might find himself out on his ear!

It also showed Charlie that the ancient royal house of Stuart had a very special place in the hearts of the people of Scotland. Actually, one of Charlie's ancestors was Robert the Bruce – a hero who won over the Scottish throne. He is so admired, he even has his own book: *Robert The Bruce And All That*.

Anyway, what you are about to read now is mostly about how the Stuarts lost everything. Some religious bits have been left out because, frankly, they are so complicated they would make your brain hurt!

Besides, the events that follow were enough to make Charlie realise what he had to do with his life . . .

SO A BLOODY WAR BROKE OUT BETWEEN KING JAMES' ARMY AND KING BILLY'S ARMY. IT LASTED ABOUT THREE YEARS AND WENT LIKE THIS...

ROUND 1 BATTLE OF KILLIECRANKIE, 1689. KING JAMES' ARMY HAD THIS ONE ALL SEWN UP UNTIL ITS LEADER GOT HIMSELF SHOT IN THE BACK BY A STRAY MUSKET BALL. (IF ONLY HE'D BEEN REACHING DOWN TO TIE HIS SHOE-LACE AT THE TIME...)

ROUND 2

BATTLE OF THE BOYNE, 1690. KING BILLY'S ARMY WON THIS BLOODY CONTEST IN IRELAND AND A FEW OTHERS BESIDES.

SCOTLAND

IRELAND

ENGLAND

ROUND 3

THE MASSACRE OF GLENCOE 1692.

A BUNCH OF JAMES' DIE-HARD FANS — THE MACDONALD CLAN OF GLENCOE — WERE WRAPPED UP IN THEIR KILTS AND ASLEEP IN THE GLEN.

THEN FRIENDS OF KING BILLY, THE CAMPBELL CLAN, TURNED UP AND SKEWERED THEM.

FINAL SCORE
3-0
TO KING BILLY

KING JAMES' OTHER SUPPORTERS GULPED WHEN THEY HEARD THE AWFUL NEWS OF THE MASSACRE OF GLENCOE.

THEY DECIDED TO LIE LOW FOR A WHILE — BUT THE STUARTS NEVER GAVE UP THEIR CLAIM TO THE THRONE.

I'm still King James (VII and II)!

ALL THIS TIME, JAMES HAD BEEN LIVING IN FRANCE WITH HIS WIFE AND YOUNG SON, JAMES FRANCIS. THE KING OF FRANCE WAS KIND AND HELPFUL TO THE STUARTS, SO WHEN JAMES (VII + II) DIED, THE FRENCH KING AGREED TO HELP THE STUARTS GET BACK THEIR THRONE...

I announce that James Francis, son of James (VII + II) should be called James (VIII + III), new king of Scotland, England, Wales and Ireland.

THE STUARTS' FRIENDS BACK IN BRITAIN PERKED UP AT THIS NEWS AND STARTED TO PLOT. THEY WERE NOW KNOWN AS THE 'JACOBITES' — THE WORD 'JACOB' IS LATIN FOR 'JAMES' SO PEOPLE WHO SUPPORTED JAMES WERE ... JACOBITES.

ANOTHER TWO EVENTS GOT THE JACOBITES HOT UNDER THE COLLAR.

IN 1707, THE SCOTS WERE FORCED TO AGREE TO A UNION

ENGLAND and SCOTLAND ARE NOW ONE KINGDOM SIGN THIS AGREEMENT (OR ELSE) ....

IN 1714, THE ENGLISH BROUGHT ACROSS ANOTHER NEW KING FROM EUROPE.

GEORGE I (OF HANOVER, GERMANY)

THE JACOBITES IN SCOTLAND DEMANDED FOUR THINGS:

BRING BACK OUR STUART MONARCHS!

SAY NO TO HANOVERIAN KING!

SCRAP THE UNION of 1707!!

A FREE BAG OF CHEESE 'N' ONION CRISPS FOR EVERYONE WHO JOINS THE JACOBITES *

*OKAY, THEY DIDN'T WANT THIS BUT IT'S A NICE THOUGHT, ISN'T IT?

TO ACHIEVE THEIR GOALS, THE JACOBITES PLOTTED THREE
REBELLIONS, ALSO KNOWN AS UPRISINGS.
BUT THEY ALL ENDED IN DISASTER!

DISASTER 1 1708. THE MAN WHO WANTED TO BE
KING JAMES ($\overline{VIII}$ + III) (CHARLIE'S DAD) SET SAIL FROM
FRANCE FOR SCOTLAND WITH BOATS BURSTING WITH FRENCH TROOPS.
HIS FLEET WAS CHASED AWAY BY THE BRITISH ROYAL NAVY. CHARLIE'S
DAD RACED BACK TO FRANCE.

Let's try another day!

DISASTER 2 1715. A MUCH BIGGER REBELLION WAS STARTED IN
SCOTLAND. THE JACOBITE SOLDIERS WERE ITCHING FOR
A FIGHT BUT THE SCOTTISH GENERAL WAS USELESS.

AND ANYWAY, CHARLIE'S DAD ARRIVED
TOO LATE THEN WENT
HOME AGAIN. HE WAS IN
A REALLY GLOOMY MOOD.

Er, I mean backwards!

I'm depressed.

Forward, men!

DISASTER 3 1719. BY NOW, THE FRENCH KING WAS FED UP WITH
CHARLIE'S DAD SO CHARLIE'S DAD PUSHED OFF TO LIVE IN
ROME. AS SOON AS HE GOT THERE, THE KING OF SPAIN
DECIDED HE WOULD HELP WITH A REBELLION. SPANISH TROOPS WERE
SENT TO SCOTLAND BUT THEY DIDN'T GET MUCH
ENCOURAGEMENT FROM THE JACOBITES - THEY
PROBABLY DIDN'T LIKE THE RAIN EITHER.
NOW CHARLIE'S DAD HAD HAD ENOUGH.

No more rebellions for me!

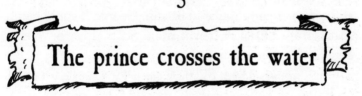

5

The prince crosses the water

So what was the moral of the story of the Jacobite Quest for young Charlie? Easy – if you want to get back your family's thrones, you need to be stronger, smarter and luckier than your hapless granddad and your hopeless dad!

Unlike his dad, Charlie was good with people, good on the battlefield and brimming with good luck. He was determined to win back the kingdoms. In fact, Charlie dreamed of raising the Stuarts' royal flag in Scotland one day and watching an army of loyal Jacobites gather round, ready for another big push. All he needed was to be given a chance . . .

Charlie's chance to win back his family's kingdoms came when France fell out with Britain's Hanoverian rulers, and the two sides went to war. When the French realised things weren't going their way, they became interested in the Jacobites again.

The French plan was to invade England, get rid of the latest Hanoverian king, George II, and replace him with our hero Charlie. Charlie would then run Britain (on behalf of his useless dad) and make sure Britain stayed friendly towards France. Hey presto!

And the chances of a Jacobite victory looked good this time. Remember, the Hanoverians were from Germany and were very unpopular in Britain. George II could barely speak proper English, never mind Scots, Irish or Welsh. People were fed up with him.

On 9 January 1744, the time came for Charlie to set sail on his quest. Before he went, he said this mouthful to his dad:

As you can see, in Charlie's day, people used a lot of words when a few would do. Just check out his dad's reply:

Without delay, Charlie jumped on a horse and rode from his home in Rome up to France. When he got there, no less than ten thousand French soldiers were ready and waiting for him. Soon Charlie and his men were on their way to Britain in a great fleet of warships.

But then disaster struck. A storm whipped the sea into a turmoil and Charlie's ships were blown off course. Many vessels were even destroyed . . . and Charlie and his men were forced to turn back.

It was not a good omen. Maybe Charlie was doomed to fail, just like his dad and granddad before him?

That's certainly what the French thought. Charlie pleaded with them to have another go, but they thought it was just too risky. So Charlie decided to go it alone. He had been preparing for this moment for most of his life and wasn't going to give up now.

Besides, Charlie knew that if he sailed to Scotland he would be welcome there. Lots of Scots hated the Hanoverians and were unhappy about the Union with England, so they would rally to his side. And Charlie reckoned that once a Jacobite rebellion in Scotland got going, the French would see sense and send a fresh army over to support him.

Charlie's dad begged his son not to try again without lots of French help. But it was too late. In July 1745 Charlie set sail again with just a handful of French troops and a sprinkling of Scottish and Irish Jacobite leaders.

Two ships made their way across the sea to Scotland, but one was met by a ship of the Royal Navy and a terrible battle followed. The Jacobite ship was forced to limp back to France. Unfortunately, it was the ship carrying most of Charlie's supplies, including lots of muskets and broadswords.

On the other hand, at least the ship carrying Charlie safely reached its destination . . .

6

Splash–landing

Charlie leapt out of the small galley that had been rowed ashore from his ship, and splashed down on a silvery beach. It was 23 July 1745, and the prince was bursting with energy and excitement at having finally arrived in Scotland.

Charlie had landed on the small isle of Eriskay in the Outer Hebrides, a remote and mysterious group of islands off Scotland's west coast. (The beach on Eriskay was later renamed Prince's Strand in honour of Charlie.)

Wading ashore alongside him were a group of Jacobites. They were the Seven Men of Somewhere We Haven't Got To Yet. Well, that's what we'll call them for now, anyway. They were a motley crew:

1. The marquis of Tullibardine, an old and sickly Scottish lord.
2. Aeneas MacDonald, a Scottish banker who didn't really want to be on the expedition at all.
3. Colonel Francis Strickland, the only Englishman in the group.
4. Sir Thomas Sheridan, an old Irish soldier.
5. Sir John MacDonald, another old-timer from Ireland who was fond of horses and even more fond of whisky.
6. Rev. George Kelly, an Irish churchman.
7. Colonel John William O'Sullivan, also from Ireland and a good fighter.

The job of the Seven Men of Somewhere We Haven't Got To Yet was to encourage other people to join Charlie's rebellion. Luckily, just about everyone on Eriskay and the neighbouring islands was a Jacobite and it was a place that the Hanoverian seamen of the Royal Navy hardly dared to set foot upon.

Like many of the surrounding islands, Eriskay was controlled by a powerful Jacobite clan called the MacDonalds of Clanranald. So Charlie had at least found a good spot to begin his rebellion, and the islanders set about making him welcome.

Or at least as welcome as they could. Eriskay could be a beautiful island in the summer, but the prince soon discovered that it could also be lashed by strong winds and rain, which suddenly made it a grey and grim place.

On top of that, the people were very poor. They ate a simple diet of milk and fish. Their homes were small, dark stone buildings with no windows. These houses were always very smoky because the islanders had only damp chunks of peat to burn on their fires to keep them warm, and no proper chimneys to let the smoke out.

So what did Charlie make of his new kingdom? He was used to living the high life in a royal palace in Rome. Surely he must have been horrified and keen to go back to his life of luxury?

Not a bit of it. Charlie was made of stronger stuff than that. He believed that a true warrior needed to be tough, so he did his best to fit in with life on the island. He even wore a beard like the island men and dressed in simple clothes – which was also a way of hiding his true identity.

Charlie even began trying to pick up the language that people spoke in the north and west of Scotland – Gaelic.

Mind you, Charlie didn't take to island life right away. On their first day, the prince and his men caught some fish that they happily roasted and ate. But they had to stay the night with a poor farmer in his simple hut.

The farmer's name was Angus MacDonald. He got very annoyed when Charlie kept complaining about the smoke in the house and going in and out for gulps of fresh air. Angus didn't understand any languages besides Gaelic and didn't realise that the awkward, secretive stranger with the beard and plain clothes was a prince. He thought Charlie was just some oddball from the continent.

'Why can't that fellow just sit still and make his mind up whether he wants to be indoors or outside?' complained Angus to the others in Gaelic.

But at least Charlie had made up his mind to start his quest, even though many of his supporters in the islands believed the time was not right.

One of the local Clanranald lords, MacDonald of Boisdale, came to visit Charlie to urge him not to continue. But Charlie was determined to carry on

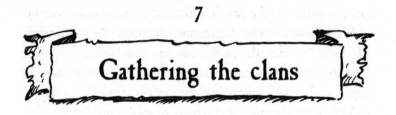

7

Gathering the clans

After spending some time on Eriskay persuading the MacDonalds of Clanranald to join the rebellion, Charlie and his small band of followers sailed to mainland Scotland. They arrived at a beautiful but wild place on the west coast called Moidart. Suddenly, the Seven Men of Somewhere We Haven't Got To Yet had a proper name . . . the Seven Men of Moidart!

Assisted by the Seven Men of Moidart, Charlie's plan was to recruit more followers from the West Highlands. But Charlie soon found that other Jacobite leaders were wary of supporting him because he didn't have a French army. So Charlie had to rely on his charm to win them over. Oh, and he also had a big chest filled with a treasure of four thousand pounds to pay any Jacobite bigwigs who fancied joining him.

Thanks to Charlie's winning personality (and his money), people began flocking to his side, including powerful clan chiefs like Donald Cameron of Lochiel. In fact, Lochiel and Charlie quickly became great friends.

Jacobite chiefs like Lochiel had hundreds, even

thousands, of clan warriors at their command. Like the MacDonalds of Clanranald before them, these clansmen were told to leave their cattle and crops – and get ready for war!

Meanwhile, in London, the Hanoverians were asleep. Well, not actually asleep, but they might as well have been. They did nothing about all the rumours that Charlie, the 'Young Pretender', had landed in Scotland to begin a rebellion against them.

The Hanoverians liked to call Charlie the Young Pretender because it made him sound less important. He wasn't a *real* heir to the thrones of Britain, they said, he was just *pretending* to be one.

Besides, the Hanoverians simply didn't believe that the Young Pretender had managed to successfully sail to Scotland. And they certainly didn't think many people would support him even if he had got there.

The Hanoverians were in for a rude awakening. Reports quickly began coming out of the Highlands that hundreds upon thousands of clan warriors were definitely on the march to join Charlie.

In August, the Hanoverians announced that they would give a reward of thirty thousand pounds (about four million pounds in today's money) for the capture of the Young Pretender. This was a huge sum of money in those days, and it shows that the Hanoverians were now very, very worried about Charlie's rebellion.

When Charlie heard there was a price on his head, he later took his revenge by announcing a reward for the capture of George II. Charlie offered just thirty pounds, which he thought was clever since it showed that George II was pretty worthless compared to him.

But everyone else laughed at Charlie for doing this. His Jacobite followers thought he was being silly and mean, because they were risking their lives for him by rebelling against George II. They said anybody who caught George II deserved a hero's reward.

Charlie eventually realised his mistake and put the price on George II up to thirty thousand, but some Jacobites had seen a side to Charlie that was daft and vain. They were worried.

Still, by now the rebellion was growing in strength and Charlie's Jacobites had had their first taste of battle. On 14 August, they captured a group of Hanoverian soldiers. But this was just a warm-up. A few days later came the moment of truth. It was time for Charlie to see exactly how many Highlanders were up for it!

The MacDonalds and the Camerons had been getting ready for war. But, to gather the clans together at his side, Charlie needed a signal that everybody would know was his. So, on 19 August, at a pretty place called Glenfinnan, near Moidart, Charlie lifted up one of his most personal possessions – which was made of silk – and held it fluttering in the breeze. In the distance, the clan warriors tried to make out what it was. Was it:

A. His hankie?
B. His royal standard?
C. His pants?

Wisely, Charlie had decided against waving his snotty hankie or sweaty pants in the air. Instead, he proudly held up his royal standard – the majestic flag that signalled Scotland's true royal family were back in business.

Before long, a large posse of clan warriors was gathered around. They were dressed in traditional Highland uniform and carried traditional Highland weapons:

- Uniform – the big kilt. This was a bigger and wilder version of the kilt people wear today. It was a six–metre–long piece of very heavy woollen cloth. Sometimes it had a simple tartan pattern, but sometimes not. You wore it by laying the cloth on the ground and making pleats in it. Then you laid down on top of it and fastened it around your body using a belt. Then you got up, took the top half of the cloth and hauled it up over your shoulders. It was fastened in place with a pin or a brooch. The clan warriors also wore bonnets. Charlie gave all his men a white ribbon to put in their bonnets, which looked like a rose he had plucked from the shores of a loch called Loch Eil. This became the Jacobite symbol and was called the **White Cockade**.

WHITE COCKADE – WHITE RIBBON IN PLACE OF CHARLIE'S WHITE ROSE

sporan – SPORRAN – PURSE

KILT

SOCKS TIED UP WITH STRAW OR TWINE

brog – BROGUES – LIGHT SHOES, GOOD FOR RUNNING ACROSS THE HEATHER

- Weapons – take your pick. If you were a clan warrior you might have had a rifle called a musket. Then you've got a few different kinds of sword to choose from. One of the most popular was the claymore. It had a small basket over the handle to protect your hand. Then there was the targe, which was a wooden shield with metal studs that you could also bash people with. Or you could always use your fists.

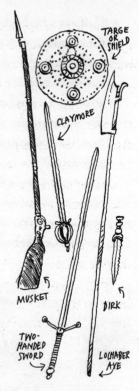

TARGE OR SHIELD

CLAYMORE

MUSKET

DIRK

TWO-HANDED SWORD

LOCHABER AXE

- Secret weapon – the bagpipes. This was, and still is, a VERY LOUD wind instrument made from sheepskin and wood. The bagpipers were always ready to raise the clansmen's spirits by giving a tune, but first . . .

Charlie gave a speech. He said that the real reason for his quest to win back his family's thrones was so he could make the people of Scotland happy. Awww, what a charmer.

According to reports, Charlie's speech was so good that the clansmen threw their bonnets in the air in approval. And the bagpipers played to celebrate the gathering of the Jacobite clans. It was a very jolly affair.

But behind all their cheering and partying, some of the clan warriors had their doubts about what they were letting themselves in for. In fact, some of them only joined Charlie's rebellion because their chiefs had turned up and threatened to burn down their cottages if they didn't!

These clansmen would have been happier staying at home and feeding their cows. They just wanted a quiet life. But there was no chance of that now.

8

Who's with us?

To keep his rebellion moving in the right direction, Charlie needed a plan. Without further ado, Charlie held a war council, or meeting, with his Jacobite leaders. The council had to decide on two important things, so they came up with an agenda. It went a bit like this:

Jacobite Council of War
Agenda
1 Strategy
2 Leadership

The first item on the agenda was strategy. This was easy to decide: 'As soon as our Jacobite force is ready, we launch a big attack on the Hanoverian government army – which is commanded by Sir John Cope – and seize Scotland.'

The second item on the agenda was leadership. More tricky. Charlie wanted to be at the top of the tree, of course, but he needed experienced generals to help him.

Once Charlie had picked a few men to help lead his army, they began the long march south to try to capture Edinburgh – Scotland's capital city. And as soon as they were on the move, the clansmen were surprised to see Charlie charging across the moors on foot.

Right away, the Highlanders could see that Charlie was no wimp like his dad. Remember, the young prince had prepared himself for war with all his hard military training. So it's not surprising that some of Charlie's soldiers were soon complaining that they couldn't keep up with him.

Yet, the longer they marched with Charlie, the more the clans *wanted* to keep up with him. They were impressed by his courage, strength and charming personality. As the Jacobite army swept through the glens, Charlie won new supporters in every village and town he passed through. And as word spread of the dashing prince and his bold quest, followers began to rise up in all sorts of places, ready to join Charlie's cause.

Just as Charlie charmed Scotland, so Scotland charmed him. This wasn't just because of the country's beautiful, wild mountain scenery. It was because of little things. For example, in Scotland the prince had his first taste of an exotic food he had never come across when he lived in Rome. Was it:

A. Pasta?
B. A pineapple?
C. A potato?

It has to be a potato, right? Wrong. In fact, Charlie tasted his first pineapple in Scotland. If it sounds ridiculous that Highlanders grew pineapples in their cold, windy back gardens, then that's because it is. Everybody knows you can't grow a pineapple in a Highland glen!

So how did the Highlanders get their hands on this exotic fruit, then? Well, pineapples were either *imported* into Scotland from warm countries far away across the ocean or they were grown in Scotland in special hothouses.

That'll be the chief's home delivery.

But pineapples are not the only surprising fact about Charlie's adventure in Scotland. Did you know, for example, that about half of Scotland's population actually lived in the Highlands in Charlie's day? This was because there weren't really any factories and industries in the Lowlands yet, like there are today. So lots of people stayed up north and worked on farms or at sea.

And did you realise that not all Highlanders supported Charlie and the Jacobites? Many Highland clans supported Charlie's enemies, the Hanoverians. They included:

1. The Campbells.   2. The Mackays.
3. The Munros.   4. The Sutherlands.

Then there were some very crafty clans who backed BOTH sides. After all, nobody knew who was going to win, so this was a kind of insurance policy. If a chief came out on the Hanoverian side, he told his sons to come out on Charlie's side. That way, depending on which side won, the clansmen could get each other out of hot water! (Or at least, that was the plan.)

And guess what else – not all Lowlanders supported the Hanoverian government. In fact, most of Charlie's army officers came from the Lowlands. And lots of Jacobite soldiers were ordinary folk from Lowland towns and villages, like shopkeepers, farmers, weavers and labourers.

So the next time somebody tells you that ALL Highlanders supported Charlie and his Jacobite rebels, but ALL Lowlanders supported Britain's Hanoverian government, you can tell them straight, 'That's a load of old rubbish!'

With friends (and enemies) rising up in all corners of the kingdom, Charlie's adventure was about to really take off . . .

9

Next stop, Edinburgh

To capture Scotland, Charlie knew he needed to march down into the Lowlands and seize control of its cities as soon as possible. But Commander Cope, the Hanoverian army leader, realised the danger. So, in late August 1745, Cope sent lots of soldiers to strengthen garrisons at the castles and forts protecting each city, while he took the rest of his men on a long march into the Highlands and up the Great Glen, towards a Hanoverian stronghold called Fort Augustus.

Cope planned to use Fort Augustus as a base for thumping the Jacobites – but Charlie was too quick for him, and was waiting to head Cope off at the pass. The Corrieyairack Pass, to be precise. Corrieyairack was not an easy word to say (by the way, it's 'Corry-ayer-ick') and not an easy place to march through, either. Especially if there's a big army of Jacobites waiting to ambush you.

Poor old Cope had been expecting that some so-called Hanoverian clans would turn up and help him blast his way through. He had even brought a thousand extra weapons for them. But his reinforcements never appeared.

So Cope decided it was too risky to try to get through to Fort Augustus. Instead, he retreated to the northern town of Inverness.

Charlie was delighted. With Cope safely out of the way, the Jacobite army was free to march south.

The march was made all the easier thanks to some unexpected help from an old Hanoverian road-builder called General Wade. After Charlie's dad's failed rebellions a few years back, General Wade had been ordered by the government to build new roads and bridges in the Highlands. The idea was that Hanoverian troops could march north quickly on these shiny new roads and give the Jacobite clans what-for if they ever decided to rebel again.

Except nobody realised that if one army can march up a road another army can also march down it. So now General Wade's handy roads were helping Charlie's army make a swift move on southern Scotland. Oops!

The Jacobite advance went smoothly, like a stagecoach that stops along the way to pick up passengers:

FIRST STOP Blair Castle. It's 31 August and Charlie's Jacobite army rolls up at this historic fortress to welcome more supporters on board. The rebels are almost in the Lowlands.

SECOND STOP Dunkeld. It's now 3 September, and by this time Charlie is so confident, he is dancing traditional Scottish dances like strathspeys to charm the public. It works.

THIRD STOP Perth, 4 September. Charlie arrives in the Lowland city with a fanfare. He proclaims his dad King James VIII of Scotland and himself Prince Regent of the Kingdom, which is a fancy way of saying, 'I'll take charge since my dad's not around.' Charlie is joined by a general called Lord George Murray. This is good news because Murray is very clever and brave, but it's also bad news when the prince upsets his other generals by making Murray his top general. Soon Charlie discovers that Murray disagrees with him about a lot of things. There may be trouble ahead. To make things worse, even the ordinary foot-soldiers are grumbling, too, because Charlie has run out of money to pay their wages. But Charlie's men have barely a moment to start complaining before . . .

FINAL STOP Edinburgh! On 17 September, the prince leads his army into the capital and boldly makes himself at home in the royal palace of Holyroodhouse. Everyone in his army is cheered up. Although Edinburgh is supposed to be a loyal Hanoverian city, next to nobody puts up a fight. This makes the Hanoverian government in England suspicious that even so-called loyal Scots are *secretly* rooting for Charlie.

So what on earth were the Hanoverian army doing while Charlie was conquering Scotland with ease? Were Cope and his men still up in Inverness, quivering with fear? Actually, no, they were now on their way south to try to find a good spot to challenge Charlie's army to a fight.

To be fair to the Hanoverians, we shouldn't forget that they not only had to deal with Charlie & Co., they were also at war with the French. That meant lots of Hanoverian soldiers were away fighting the French in a place next door to France called the Austrian Netherlands (which today is called Belgium), instead of being in Britain to take on the Jacobites.

All of which left Charlie free to bask in glory in Edinburgh for as long as he liked – or at least until Commander Cope got his act together. As Charlie puffed up the silk cushions on his king-sized bed in Holyroodhouse, he got used to a life of luxury again. And he got used to being the talk of the town.

At just twenty-four, Charlie had suddenly become a legend in his own lifetime. He was a dashing rebel, a real-life fairytale prince – tall, fit, charming and handsome. If celebrity magazines had been around then, Charlie would have been on the cover of every one.

Wherever he went, Charlie went down a storm, especially with the ladies. Crowds of beauties gathered outside the palace windows. They even threw their handkerchiefs onto the ground, each one hoping the heart-stopping prince would appear to reach down and pick theirs up – a sign that he wanted to become their boyfriend.

Some girls were more persistent. They pushed their way into the palace to kiss the prince's hand. Like a famous film star or pop idol, Charlie was everyone's darling.

He certainly dressed the part. The prince wore a fancy tartan coat, a light-coloured wig and a blue bonnet. In the evenings, Charlie held balls and parties at the palace, giving the ladies another chance to ogle him – and perhaps even to have the honour of a dance.

With all this female attention, Charlie's troops began to notice a change in him. The tough, macho soldier many of them had met at Glenfinnan was becoming a softer, more dandyish fellow. It was almost as though fame was going to Charlie's head.

His soldiers didn't complain too much, mind you, when Charlie's popularity earned him extra cash to pay their wages. The lords and ladies of Edinburgh and Perth loved him so much they gave him loans to help pay for his army, or else donated cash to his cause.

Although he pranced about Edinburgh impressing the ladies, deep down Charlie knew he was on a mission. On 18 September, he ordered a thousand tents, six thousand pairs of shoes and six thousand canteens – little containers of water and cutlery for cooking. So were Charlie and his men going on a camping trip? Well, not exactly . . .

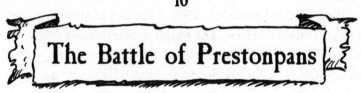

10

The Battle of Prestonpans

Charlie's order for new equipment also included two thousand targes. These sturdy wooden shields meant only one thing – it was time for a battle.

The prince heard that Commander Cope was waiting for him to the east of Edinburgh, at a place called Prestonpans. Charlie knew that Scotland could not be conquered properly until the Hanoverians' Scottish army was defeated. So, on 20 September, he rallied his men with words of encouragement and marched into battle.

Good old tough-guy Charlie was back, and he wanted to lead his army from the front. Only his generals wouldn't let him. If the prince was killed or captured, they said, the whole Jacobite cause would be doomed. Reluctantly, Charlie agreed.

When they reached Prestonpans, another thing Charlie and his generals argued over was picking the best spot to camp the Jacobite army in before the battle. The disagreements were bad-tempered, and Charlie and Murray fell out over it. This was not a good omen for the future.

But at least they agreed on launching a surprise attack on Commander Cope, early in the morning of 21 September. The plan was for Lochiel and his clansmen to do a

Highland Charge. This famous manoeuvre is one you can practise, with the help of a volunteer, in your garden:

1. Run at your enemy with your eyes wide open, screaming your head off.
2. Watch your enemy run away in terror.

As the crazed-looking clansmen rushed forward, the first to flee from Commander Cope's side were his cavalry. This was pretty pathetic, since cavalry were mounted on horses, with lots of fancy armour and fine weapons. But, to be fair, the Highland Charge *was* terrifying. Charlie watched the Hanoverian cavalry gallop away and wrote a note to his father saying they 'ran like rabets'. What he meant to write was 'rabbits', but, like many people in the 1700s, Charlie hadn't got the hang of spelling yet.

As for Commander Cope's foot-soldiers, they had no way to escape. The poor devils were hacked, stabbed, slashed and skewered by the charging Jacobite Highlanders.

The cornfields under the soldiers' feet were turned red by blood and guts. Arms, legs and heads were sent flying all over the place as sword blades cut through everything in their path. Around three hundred Hanoverians were splattered and about five hundred were wounded. Compare that to Charlie's side – only about twenty Jacobites were killed and around fifty injured.

It was a great victory to the Jacobites, but Charlie wasn't happy about all the death and gore. So he ordered his men not to kill any more of the enemy, but to take them prisoner instead. And he told his surgeons to look after the enemy wounded.

This was Charlie showing his honourable side. As far as he was concerned, even enemy soldiers were still his subjects – and his dad was their king. They had been either fooled or forced into fighting against him by their Hanoverian masters. So they deserved to be given a second chance. That was how Charlie saw it, anyway.

The battle of Prestonpans proved to the Hanoverian government in London that Charlie meant business. Poor Commander Cope was devastated by his failure and Scotland was now a Stuart kingdom again. Well, almost.

Remember the ship that had been lost on the way over from France, carrying most of Charlie's supplies? On board had been Charlie's artillery – his cannons and other big guns. He needed these to smash the stone walls of Scotland's really big castles and capture them from the Hanoverians.

But without his artillery Charlie had been forced to steer well clear. So, for example, although Charlie controlled Edinburgh, he wasn't the king of Edinburgh Castle. It was still full of Hanoverians. A number of other big castles were the same.

EDINBURGH CASTLE – FULL OF HANOVERIANS

FIRTH OF FORTH

PRESTONPANS

CITY OF EDINBURGH – IN CHARLIE'S HANDS

HOLYROOD PALACE

HANOVERIANS FLEE FROM HERE

This was not good. If a fresh Hanoverian army turned up to relieve these castle garrisons, Charlie would be in big trouble.

But for now, the prince savoured the taste of his first major victory and returned to Edinburgh to decide on his next move . . .

11

So what next?

Charlie now faced the first of many difficult decisions. Should he stay and rule Scotland or else try to take control of England and the rest of Britain as well? The prince decided to have another war council, which met every day in his privy (private) chamber.

Personally, Charlie wanted to invade England, but he was wise enough to hear the views of his Jacobite generals on the matter first. As soon as the meetings got going, though, he wished he'd never bothered. Very quickly, Charlie and Murray fell out again over what to do next and formed two gangs.

More Jacobites joined Murray's gang than joined Charlie's, which made Charlie very angry. Some of those on Charlie's side began whispering that Murray was a traitor who would one day betray the prince.

The arguments between Charlie and Murray were very angry, and went a bit like this:

Charlie refused to listen to Murray and fought hard to get his plan to invade England agreed by the Jacobite council. As far as Charlie was concerned, his quest didn't end in Scotland. His family were the rightful kings of all three kingdoms in the British Isles and he wouldn't rest until they got *all* their crowns back.

But a lot of Scottish Jacobites were unhappy about marching south, not just Murray. They weren't really interested in conquering England. They wanted the Union of 1707 to be scrapped and Scotland to become a separate kingdom again.

But whenever anyone asked Charlie what he planned to do about the Union, he was very vague about it. One minute he hinted that he would get rid of it, the next minute he said he would prefer to just change it to somehow make it better. To the Scots, it all sounded a bit fishy.

When the day to begin the long march into England arrived, most Jacobite soldiers would have been quite happy to just stay in bed. Especially since it was Hallowe'en – a time when people believed evil spirits stalked the land. But not even the Devil himself could have kept Charlie from the gates of London.

So the Jacobite army waved goodbye to the people of Edinburgh and, a few days later, crossed the border. They spent their first night in England on 8 November.

To perk his men up, Charlie went back to his tough-guy routine. He didn't ride a horse, but preferred to make his way on foot alongside the ordinary clansmen.

'Watch this, he'll put on this heroic show for a day or two and then go back to being a dandy on horseback,' said the doubters.

But Charlie proved the doubters wrong. According to reports, the prince marched at the head of his men, day after day, along dirty tracks and through deep snow. He even went back to help the stragglers who were struggling to keep up and, at night, he was so tough he slept with his boots on.

Meanwhile, the Hanoverians had appointed a new commander of their army. It was Wade, the road-builder whose magnificent military roads had . . . er, just helped the Jacobites zip right through Scotland.

In fact, old Field-Marshall Wade, as he was now called, seemed to be a bit of a jinx as far as the Hanoverians were concerned. Wade was meant to stop Charlie getting his hands on the important northern English town of Carlisle, but he was too slow and too late. Charlie waltzed into the town on 18 November with barely a spot of bother.

As the Jacobites continued their march south, the weather got pretty grim. Snow, sleet and ice nipped the faces, fingers and feet of Charlie and his men. But their hearts were warm after toppling their first English town and soon others followed suit – Penrith, Lancaster, Preston and Manchester. London was getting nearer and nearer.

Wherever he went in England, Charlie charmed the pants off just about everyone. Again, the ladies loved him.

But there was a problem. Although hardly anybody seemed to be against the prince and lots of people seemed to like him, very few English Jacobites actually signed up to join Charlie's army. They thought it was just too risky.

Charlie didn't think this was a major problem, since it seemed like the Hanoverian army had just given up and gone away. On 4 December, the Jacobites entered Derby, again without anybody putting up a fight. Charlie was now getting close to London, which was just 120 miles away. His men could march there in about five days. Surely nothing could stop Charlie now?

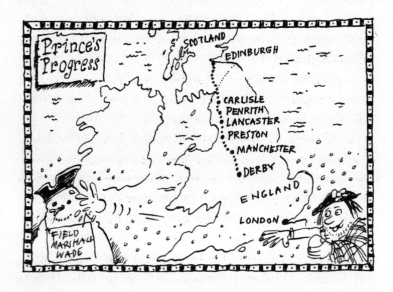

12

The moment of truth

To march on London would be to take a huge gamble – the biggest of Charlie's life so far. He was willing to take the chance that the Hanoverian city guards would crumble as soon as they saw his army of rebels. He could then stroll through the city and seize the English throne.

But to be a successful gambler, you need to convince your supporters that you're going to win. And Charlie didn't do a very good job of that.

It all came down to trust – or rather, lack of it. Charlie had been saying for ages that the English Jacobites would rise up and join the rebellion. It never happened. And he had been saying right from the start that the French would send over an army to help out. That never happened, either.

Murray and many of the Jacobite chiefs had had enough of Charlie's broken promises. They were now deep in enemy territory, a long, long way from home. And they were on their own. No French troops, next to no English Jacobites . . . just a small army of hungry and exhausted Scottish rebels.

Feeling small and vulnerable, Murray and the others began to get really paranoid that the force guarding London must be really huge. The Hanoverians were just ready and waiting for them to march into the trap, Murray thought, where they would be crushed like porridge oats in a mill.

Again, Charlie got very angry with Murray and said he was being a coward. Charlie was convinced that if the Jacobites carried on with their attack the Londoners wouldn't know what had hit them. He pleaded with his men to be bold and go for it.

But Murray and his gang dug their heels in and refused. They thought Charlie's dream of becoming king had gone to his head. They reckoned that only a madman would march on London without more muscle on his side.

So who was right? Well, actually . . . it was Charlie.

The prince's hunch that the Jacobites could capture London was a good one. While some Hanoverians were either too dozy to care about the Jacobite army camped up the road in Derby, others were frozen with fear. Either way, the Hanoverians were in no state to put up a fight.

One leading Hanoverian in London, the duke of Richmond, wrote to one of his friends that:

> *...The whole kingdom is asleep. Our cavalry can't be here before February and the Pretender may be crowned in Westminster by that time...*

If only such letters had fallen into Charlie's hands, then he would have been able to *prove* to Murray and the other doubters that victory was theirs for the taking. But it was not to be. Instead, Charlie lost the argument and the order was given to retreat.

On Friday 6 December, the Jacobite army turned around and began its long march north. It became known as Black Friday – the worst day of Charlie's life. He felt like his so-called Jacobite followers had betrayed him, wrenching the English crown away just as it was within his grasp.

But if Murray and his pals thought that retreat would get the Jacobites out of harm's way, they were wrong. In fact, the dangerous part of the mission was just about to begin . . .

13

The longest road

Until now, Charlie had marched at the front of his army with his head held high. But as the Jacobites were retreating from Derby with their tails between their legs, Charlie lost his appetite for leading them. He rode a horse at the rear of his men, hanging his head in despair.

While Charlie sulked, Murray and the others convinced each other they were doing the right thing. 'All we need to do is get back to Scotland,' they said to themselves. 'We can hide in the Highlands for the winter and rest, and then have another go in the spring.'

Murray reckoned that the only obstacle blocking the 500-mile road to Scotland was Field-Marshall Wade. But he was wrong.

A new Hanoverian commander had been ordered to hunt down the prince. His name was William Augustus, Duke of Cumberland, youngest son of the Hanoverian king, George II.

Like Charlie, Cumberland was eager to prove himself to his dad. And, just as Charlie had been, he was also popular with his own men. But unlike Charlie, Cumberland was extremely ruthless and bloodthirsty with his enemies. He enjoyed splattering people.

With Cumberland in hot pursuit, the Jacobites waded over the River Esk on 20 December and raced towards Scotland. Charlie crossed the border on his twenty-fifth birthday. For a couple of weeks, at least, he was safe. But the garrison he left behind to try to hold Carlisle Castle for him was not so lucky.

Before long, Cumberland turned up in Carlisle. To show the Jacobite garrison what he had in store for them, Cumberland took four quivering Jacobites he had captured earlier and hanged them outside the castle walls until they were dead.

Then Cumberland battered, blasted and broke apart the walls of the castle with his cannons. Eventually, the Jacobites surrendered and Cumberland divided them into two groups, with two different punishments:

Cumberland was more ruthless than a rottweiler in a litter of kittens – and he wanted everyone to know it. What's more, he was only just getting started. He planned to do even worse things when he got his hands on the rest of the Jacobites.

Meanwhile, Charlie and his men barely had any time to celebrate New Year 1746 – not that there was much to celebrate. By early January, another Hanoverian force, led by Lieutenant-General Henry Hawley, was out to get them.

Luckily, even though the Jacobites' heads were down, Hawley hardly had a clue how to win battles. When Charlie's Jacobites charged against Hawley's Hanoverians outside the town of Falkirk on 17 January, it ended in an easy victory for the rebels. After that, the Jacobites went on to capture Stirling. Things were looking up.

What Charlie should have done next was take heart from this victory and go and capture Edinburgh (which had fallen back into Hanoverian hands while the Jacobites were in England). But Charlie was still in a huff about being forced to turn back at Derby. In fact, ever since the going got tough, he seemed to be becoming more and more like his hopeless dad.

Charlie was so gloomy and upset about his situation that he made himself sick. This was not surprising – when you're full of beans and you think positive, like Charlie did on the march south, it's good for your health. When you're droopy and in despair, like Charlie was now, it's bad for your health, and you pick up bugs and colds more easily.

Charlie tried to cheer himself up by finding a girlfriend.

Her name was Clementina Walkinshaw, the daughter of a Jacobite lord. Clementina really cared about Charlie and nursed him while he was unwell.

But Charlie had changed. He began wearing fancy royal costumes instead of dressing like a soldier in simple clothes and hard military boots, like he had done before. And, when he wasn't feeling sick, he preferred singing and dancing to planning his next move with his generals. It was as though Charlie had given up on his quest – even though it was far from over and there was still a chance of success!

To get things back on track, Murray and his pals in the Jacobite leadership argued their case again:

Murray was right to be worried about Cumberland. The Hanoverian duke was now on his way into Scotland and growing more and more determined to give the rebels a good thrashing.

As for Charlie, he didn't want to retreat any further. He *still* kept insisting that the French would send an army. This was not just Charlie being daft. The French really were thinking about sending an army over, it's just that instead of actually *doing it* they kept thinking . . . and thinking . . . and thinking about it.

That wasn't good enough for Murray and the others. They didn't want to risk staying in the Lowlands. So Charlie was outvoted, yet again.

By now, Charlie's relationship with Murray was frostier than a snowflake on a frozen loch. So the retreat into the Highlands on 1 February was an exceptionally chilly one! But, when the Jacobites eventually got into the Highlands, at least they still had the strength to capture some important strongholds, like Fort Augustus and Inverness.

Meanwhile, Cumberland was crawling up the east coast of Scotland. He seized important towns on the coast like Perth and Aberdeen. His plan was to make it as difficult as possible for any ships that might come with Jacobite soldiers from France to find a port where they could safely land.

Cumberland couldn't chase Charlie's army into the Highlands, though, because he was blocked by the River Spey. Its waters were too high and fast-running to cross safely due to the melting winter snow and ice gushing down from the mountains.

But that did not mean the Jacobites were clear of danger. Charlie had run out of money to pay his soldiers (again). What's more, the prince became sick with stress (again).

And now that they were back in their homelands, the clansmen began deserting.

As though all that were not bad enough, the waters of the River Spey slowly began to get lower, and lower, and lower . . .

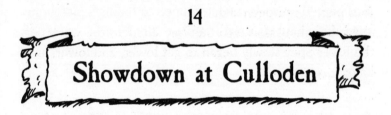

14

Showdown at Culloden

On 12 April, Cumberland's army splashed across the Spey and began making their way towards Inverness. Meanwhile, Charlie's army was camped at a spot east of Inverness, trying to decide what to do next. When the Jacobites heard the news that Cumberland was on his way, Murray tried to make peace with Charlie by offering three suggestions:

STRATEGY

1 RETURN TO INVERNESS AND DEFEND IT AGAINST CUMBERLAND.

2 SPLIT UP – HEAD FOR THE MOUNTAINS – HIDE OUT – LAUNCH SMALL, SURPRISE ATTACKS.

3 FIGHT CUMBERLAND IN BIG BATTLE ON GOOD SPOT SOUTH OF RIVER NAIRN.

Charlie's response? 'No', 'No' and 'No'. Trying to defend Inverness was too risky, he said. Heading for the hills would leave the men with nothing to eat, he said. And fighting south of the River Nairn would make it easy for Cumberland to just march right past them and capture Inverness, he said.

This time Murray would not win the argument – Charlie had perked up and was determined to follow a plan of his own. So what was Charlie's plan, then?

A. PICK A REALLY EXCELLENT SPOT FOR A BATTLE WHERE THE JACOBITES SIMPLY CAN'T LOSE.

OR B. PICK A DREADFUL SPOT FOR A BATTLE WHERE JACOBITES ARE FACED WITH ALMOST CERTAIN DEATH.

Yup, you guessed it – Charlie somehow went for option B. He chose a field to the east of Inverness called Culloden. Culloden was in a place called Drumossie Moor – a great big, boggy marshland.

With its wet ground and bushy heather, Culloden was extremely difficult to run across. This meant the Jacobite clans couldn't attack the enemy with a proper Highland Charge – their strongest weapon. Basically, Charlie couldn't have picked a worse place to fight if he tried.

So what was Charlie thinking? Had he lost the plot? That's what Murray thought, but Charlie believed Culloden was the best place to stop Cumberland in his tracks. The prince was determined to stop the Hanoverians reaching Inverness. Besides, he had grown to hate the Hanoverian duke and he was itching to have a showdown. And Charlie had a trick up his sleeve.

On the night before the agreed day of battle, Charlie sent most of his soldiers out to launch a surprise attack on

Cumberland's sleeping soldiers. But disaster struck! Dawn broke before the Jacobites had time to reach Cumberland's camp and they had to rush back before the enemy saw them. This left Charlie's soldiers exhausted. It was another boob by the prince.

On the morning of 16 April 1746 Charlie's tired, hungry and ragged army of six thousand Jacobites took to the field at Culloden and waited for their Hanoverian enemies. It was a horrible day, as though even the weather wanted to join in the fight. A cold wind chilled every bone in every Jacobite body, while hailstones drummed against their frozen cheeks.

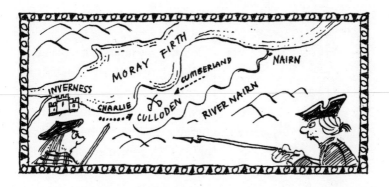

Then, after what seemed like an eternity, the Hanoverian soldiers began to trudge into view at around eleven o'clock in the morning. There were nine thousand of them, many dressed in smart uniforms with bright red coats. The army included Hawley and his men.

The Jacobites could see from all the flags and banners that the Hanoverian side was supported by three tough

Scottish regiments. The Jacobites could also see that the Hanoverians had quite a few cannons. Loads of muskets, too. And plenty of ammunition. Gulp.

The Jacobites tried to hide their fear by looking as mean and menacing as possible. Their tartans and kilts flared in the wind, their claymores and metal-studded targes glinted in the dull grey light and their bonnets still bore the White Cockade.

Er... not yet...

In a flash, the battle started, with Cumberland's cannons pounding the ground around the Jacobites. The Jacobite regiments waited for the order to charge. They waited . . . and waited . . .

While Hanoverian guns cracked off their loads in plumes of smoke, Charlie held back from giving the order to charge. 'What's he waiting for?' the Jacobite soldiers wondered as the cannonballs and other artillery rained down on them.

Charlie was too far back to properly see what was going on. He didn't think the time was right to charge yet. Murray, on the other hand, had different ideas.

Murray called on the prince to give the order for a Highland Charge so the Jacobites could attack. Eventually, the order was given: 'Claymore!' But the boy whose job it was to tell everyone had his head blown off by a cannon ball – so many Jacobites still didn't know what was going on and launched their charges too late. The Highland Charge had to be well organised to succeed, but this time it was a mess.

The Highlanders hurdled over the bushy heather and staggered across the marshy bog as best they could. They managed to protect themselves from being attacked from the front with their targes.

But, because the Jacobites were all running forward at different times, it was easy work for the Hanoverians to shoot at them from the side. And when the Jacobites were too close to shoot, the Hanoverians simply skewered every Jacobite that tried to go past them in the side of his ribs.

Some Jacobites hadn't even begun their charge yet. They *still* didn't know what was going on. So Murray fought his way back to try to get them going, but, when he turned around to look for them, his heart sank.

The White Cockades were leaving the field – and so was the prince. Charlie reckoned the battle was heading for disaster and decided to retreat.

'Run, you cowardly Italian!' shouted one of the Jacobite commanders at Charlie, as the prince galloped away.

In less than an hour after it began, the Battle of Culloden was all over. It was Charlie's first defeat. But, boy, was it a bad one . . .

15

The Butcher and the Hangman

The bodies of a thousand Jacobites lay strewn about on the battlefield at Culloden. But that wasn't enough for the victorious Hanoverian duke. He had a plan that would earn him the nickname Butcher Cumberland. So what was it?

A. Open up a butcher's shop and sell meat to starving Jacobites at affordable prices.

B. Hunt down every last Jacobite and slice them up like sausages.

Yes, that's right. Butcher Cumberland wasn't much of a businessman, and he went for Plan B. And he was helped by Hawley, who also found a nickname – Hangman Hawley. Hmmm . . . Hawley probably didn't earn that one by being nice to the Jacobites, either.

Now that Charlie's army was defeated, Hanoverian redcoats were sent out into the Jacobite glens with instructions on what to do. They went a bit like this:

> **Upon finding a Jacobite, you must:-**
>
> 1 Burn down his house (preferably with him+family inside).
> 2 Chase away his cattle
> 3 Sink his boat
>
> **Upon finding a Jacobite you think might possibly have a Weapon, you must:-**
>
> 1 Shoot him.
> 2 Shoot him again, just to make sure.

The redcoats and other Hanoverian soldiers followed their orders to the letter. When they found thirty Jacobite officers hiding in a barn, they didn't bother telling anyone to come out with their hands up – they just barricaded the door, torched the barn and roasted the Jacobites alive. Ugh!

The only way to escape the slaughter was to run for the hills, which is exactly what Charlie was doing . . .

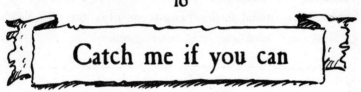

16

Catch me if you can

Charlie was running, but he was no coward. Sure, he had made a mess of Culloden, but there was no sense in staying to be slaughtered. He had to flee in order to keep the Jacobite cause alive.

The prince knew that if he was killed or captured, the dreams of his most loyal followers would be in ruins. All the soldiers who had stuck with him through thick and thin would have made their sacrifices for nothing. By escaping now, at least Charlie would live to fight another day. He could always launch another rebellion later.

Charlie sent out messengers with letters for Murray and the other Jacobite commanders, who were trying to gather together the Jacobite survivors at a place called Ruthven. Charlie's letters told them them that this rebellion was now officially over. It was every man for himself.

Murray sent Charlie an angry reply accusing him of treachery, but Charlie didn't have time to worry about that. The Hanoverians still had a price of thirty thousand pounds on his head. Charlie needed to find a way of escaping over the sea to France before he was caught – or somebody turned him in.

The 1745–46 Jacobite rebellion was over, but Charlie's greatest adventure was only just beginning . . .

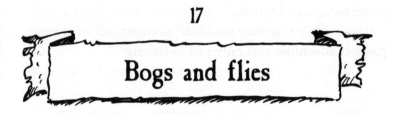

17

Bogs and flies

With redcoats hot on his tail, the prince fled through the heather and across the hills to the west coast. To get away as quickly as possible without being seen, Charlie rested in hideouts during the day and travelled at night under cover of darkness.

When he got the coast, Charlie took a boat to the very place where his Scottish adventure had begun – the islands of the Outer Hebrides. But he couldn't shake off his pursuers, and they crossed the Sea of the Hebrides to give chase.

It was a game of cat and mouse. Hanoverian forces in boats searched the shores and bays of the islands for the prince, while others hunted for him in the hills. No stone was left unturned.

Charlie spent a lot of time hiding out on the islands of South Uist and Benbecula. These islands were, and still are, beautiful but harsh places. They were barren and rugged, and swarming with clouds of tiny flies called midges. These bloodsuckers chased after Charlie and he had scars for years later because of their bites.

Which are worse – redcoats or midges?

And there were other hazards. The bog on Benbecula was so deep and marshy it sucked Charlie's shoes off! He had to run about barefoot after that until he could get a new pair.

But being sucked into the bog and chased by flies were the least of Charlie's worries. One day, on the island of South Uist, the prince was making his way across a hill when he thought he spotted a Hanoverian ship coming towards the island, so he scrambled down to the shoreline and crept into a crack in the rocks called the Hidden Harbour.

Once safely deep inside, Charlie braced his back and feet against either wall until he got comfortable, then pulled his bonnet down over his head and drank some brandy to warm his spirits until the danger passed.

Of course, Charlie knew he couldn't keep hiding in caves forever. He was trying to stay out of harm's way just long enough for word to reach France that he was in peril. The French would then send a boat to come and get him and he would escape to safety . . . he hoped.

So, to keep out of danger until then, Charlie had to keep moving. The Outer Hebrides were becoming too dangerous to stay in. But if Charlie was to find another place to hide, he would need some help.

Luckily, the MacDonalds who ruled the islands were just as loyal to the prince as they had always been. Even the man who was supposed to be leading the Hanoverian search for Charlie on South Uist was a secret Jacobite! His name was Hugh MacDonald of Armadale.

Hugh told Charlie that he could get him back over the sea to a hideout on the island of Skye. But it wouldn't be easy. Charlie was instructed to go to a hut at midnight on 21 June, where he would meet the agent who was going to smuggle him to safety.

When he walked into the hut, the prince might have been surprised by what he saw . . .

An island fling

If Charlie had been expecting a rough and ready clan warrior to rescue him, he was in for a shock. Instead, Charlie came face to face with Hugh's 24-year-old step-daughter, Flora MacDonald.

Like Charlie, Flora was a bit of a looker. She had taken some persuading beforehand to help the prince. But when she met him she was charmed. Then she got down to business, and she gave Charlie two options:

Option one: You get dressed up as a woman and pretend to be my Irish maid. Your new name will be Betty Burke. This disguise will make you look silly but it is the best way to get you over to Skye without being caught.

While I am getting your costume and passport, you will have to sleep outside in the heather.

The forecast is rain, I'm afraid!

Option two... What's so bad about option one?

Reluctantly, Charlie realised option one was his only choice. A week later, on 27 June, Charlie's dinner was interrupted with the news that Hanoverian troops were getting close. Time to put on his new disguise and get going!

Charlie was just about to strap on his pistol when he was told to forget about it. If the Hanoverians stopped and searched 'Betty' and found a gun, they would know right away who *he* really was.

Flora and her maid 'Betty' set sail the next day. But the weather was stormy, making it a very rough crossing. And as they got near Skye new dangers appeared. A Hanoverian ship spotted them and started to shoot, but it couldn't catch them.

This journey was so dramatic, a famous song was written about it years later called 'The Skye Boat Song':

Speed bonny boat like a bird on the wing, 'Onward!'
    the sailors cry.
Carry the lad who's born to be king, over the sea
    to Skye!

When the bonnie boat safely landed on Skye with Flora and 'Betty', one or two folk were a bit suspicious that 'Betty' seemed very manly for a maid. But just as it looked like Charlie was about to be found out, he was rescued when Flora handed him on to yet another MacDonald supporter, called MacDonald of Kingsburgh.

Kingsburgh gave the prince a safe place to stay, where he ate a nice meal and had a long sleep in a comfy bed. It was the first time he had done this for ages. In the morning, Charlie dressed as a man again and walked into the main village on Skye, called Portree.

There, Charlie met Flora for the very last time. The prince kissed her hand, thanked her and said goodbye.

Some people think Charlie was very sad that he had to leave because there had been a bit of romance between him and Flora. There is no evidence they fancied each other, but then again, who knows?

19

Cluny's Cage

On 5 July, Charlie made the short hop by boat from Skye to the mainland. It wasn't long before Cumberland found out where Charlie was, though, and he sent fifteen hundred redcoats to try to capture him. The 30,000-pound reward was still up for grabs.

With redcoats swarming all over the place, one wrong move and Charlie would be caught for sure. The Hanoverian soldiers got so close to the prince's hiding places at times he could even hear what they were chatting about!

Luckily, Charlie still had a lot of loyal followers on the mainland, too, who wanted to help him. They ignored the huge reward they could earn for handing over the prince *and* ignored the risk of certain death if the government found out they were helping him escape.

One of these loyal friends was called Cluny MacPherson. Cluny took Charlie to the ultimate hiding place – a special cage hidden in a remote mountain called Ben Alder.

Cluny's Cage was a hideout on two storeys. The upper room was where Cluny and Charlie slept. The lower room was where they ate. The view out allowed them to see any enemies that might approach. The entrance was hidden by thick holly and guards were posted outside. It was perfect.

For days, Charlie hid in Cluny's Cage until a messenger came with news that a ship from France was on its way to rescue him. At last, the French had kept a promise! So Charlie left Cluny's Cage and headed west, to a place near where he had first arrived in mainland Scotland.

On 20 September, after five months on the run, Charlie stepped on board the waiting French ship. He was on his way back to France, at last. As for Cluny, he stayed behind in Scotland with instructions to make preparations.

Preparations? What preparations? Well, Charlie planned to be back soon with a new army . . .

20

The hero returns

When Charlie reached France, he discovered his adventure in Britain had made him the most famous man in Europe. Everywhere he went, crowds gathered on the streets to cheer him.

They thought Charlie was a hero for being brave enough to lead a rebellion in the first place, and especially because of his miraculous escape. The prince was invited to parties, so rich ladies could meet the hero and swoon while he told of his adventures.

October 1746 seemed like the high point of Charlie's life. Except, deep down, Charlie didn't feel like a hero. He felt like a failure and didn't want to be admired. His mission had not been a success and many ordinary folk had died in vain trying to help him make his dream come true.

Charlie was determined to become a real hero by having another go. So he begged the French king, Louis XV, to give him an army so he could start a new rebellion. But Louis refused.

Charlie became very depressed about his predicament. He started drinking lots of brandy to take his mind off things, but this only made him very drunk and even more sad. And he fell out with his brother Henry, because Henry also refused to help start another rebellion. Henry decided to be a cardinal in the Catholic Church instead.

Charlie kept trying to persuade the French to change their minds, but when France decided to make peace with Britain's Hanoverian rulers in 1748 the game was up. The French would never help Charlie now.

Worse still, the French could hardly allow someone like Charlie to stay in their country now that they had made up with the Hanoverians. So he was politely asked to leave.

As you can imagine, Charlie felt utterly betrayed. He just couldn't believe that people who had once been his friends could leave him in the lurch like that. So he refused to go. And he carried on his life in France as usual until, one day, while he was on his way to see an opera, the French police arrested him. Charlie didn't like the idea of going to jail, so eventually he agreed to pack his bags.

But where would he go? He was too embarrassed about failing his mission to go back and face his dad in Rome. Instead, Charlie would have to go on the run again . . .

21

On the run again

No matter where he went, as long as Charlie lived he was a threat to the Hanoverians. So he was sure they were still out to get him. And he was right.

To stay safe while he tried to find a new home, Charlie became very good at skulking about wearing a disguise. He used lots of bits and bobs to disguise himself:

A false nose.

A wig.

Black priestly robes.

Black dye for his eyebrows and beard.

Wearing his disguises, Charlie skulked his way through Switzerland, Germany and the Low Countries (Holland and Belgium). He even went back to France a few times.

Not only that but Charlie dared to cross the Channel and visit London for a while in 1750. He thought that the Hanoverian King George II was at death's door and planned to grab his crowns by surprise. Unfortunately for Charlie, George got better and lived for another ten years. Drat!

Charlie's disguises could fool most people, but not everyone. After a few years, a Hanoverian spy began following him and writing reports about what he was up to. The spy was called Pickle. To avoid getting in a pickle with Pickle, Charlie had to stay one step ahead. So Charlie used lots of false names. Some were ordinary:

- Mr Benn
- Mr Douglas
- Mr Thompson

Some were fancy:

- Dumont
- Cartouche

And one was probably chosen by Charlie while he was drunk . . .

- The Wild Man

To confound Pickle and other Hanoverian spies even more, Charlie was helped by lots of impersonators who pretended to be him. Charlie hadn't asked to be impersonated, it's just that people thought he was such a celebrity they wanted to be in his shoes. This was very handy for the prince. The Hanoverians might arrest 'Charlie' – but how could they be sure they had the right man?

22

End of the road

The real Charlie eventually returned to Rome in 1766, after his dad died. Once there, Charlie lived in the place where it had all started, the Palazzo Muti.

Now that his dad was gone, Charlie hoped important people like the pope would call him King Charles III of Scotland, England, Wales and Ireland. This would give Charlie a chance of having one last go at winning over his crowns. But the pope refused.

Charlie was gutted. He started drinking more and more strong booze to try to make himself feel better, but it just made him feel awful. He lost his good looks and became very grumpy.

Unlike his hopeless dad, Charlie wasn't happy just kicking his heels in Rome. Charlie wanted to be out there, fighting for his dream.

People everywhere thought Charlie was a hero, but he thought he was a failure. The fact is that Charlie *was* a hero, he was just an unlucky one.

Charlie's gloomy moods made life hard for the people who loved and cared for him. Remember Clementina, the Jacobite girl Charlie had started going out with in Stirling back in 1746? After a few years apart, they had got back together. But Clementina soon found that she couldn't put up with Charlie's bad temper and decided to leave him. But at least they had had a daughter together. Her name was Charlotte.

Charlotte cared for her dad after his next romance ended in disaster too. Charlie had married a young German woman called Louise of Stolberg in 1772. But eight years later she also left Charlie and ran off with a young poet called Count Vittorio Alfieri.

After that, poor Charlie became very ill. But thanks to Charlotte's care and attention, he got better and kept going into old age.

Thanks also to Charlotte, Charlie became friends again with his brother Henry. Charlie was extremely lucky to have Charlotte's help, especially since she was seriously ill herself – with cancer.

Charlie's quest to be king was still unfinished business. But even brave adventurers like Charlie can't live forever.

On 30 January 1788, Charlie died and was buried at St Peter's church in Rome. He was sixty-eight years old. A year later, Charlotte died too.

So what became of Charlie's dream to get the Stuarts back on their thrones? Did Charlie's brother Henry pick up where Charlie had left off? Not really.

Henry claimed he was now the rightful heir to the thrones of Britain, but he didn't do much about it, and he died in 1807. Henry was the last of the royal Stuart line. There would never be another Jacobite rebellion ever again.

So does that mean Charlie took the Jacobite fighting spirit to the grave with him? Is his dream dead and buried? Oh, no. In fact, in a way, Charlie's dream of becoming a king has come true . . .

Epilogue

Charlie's life was a great success. Sure, his mum and dad didn't get on. Sure, his brother was always the favourite. And sure, he had to dress up as an old maid and wear lots of other silly disguises. But none of that stopped Charlie chasing his dream.

Instead of being a wee softie and choosing an easy life in a Roman palace, charming Charlie decided to risk it all for a shot at glory.

He didn't win back the crowns of Britain, but he was still brave enough to have a go – and that makes him a hero in anyone's book (not just this one!).

He didn't live to become a monarch, but in every other way Charlie was a true king. Especially compared with his gormless granddad, who started the Stuarts' problems by running away from the throne when the going got tough. Or his dopey dad, who was too hopeless to lead a rebellion properly when he had the chance.

Charlie didn't win the battle of Culloden, but he won all his other battles. And his enemies never caught him, because he had lots of loyal friends. These friends never betrayed him when he was on the run, no matter how big a reward was offered. That's because Charlie had a special place in people's hearts – and he still does.

Not like his enemies. Butcher Cumberland is remembered only as a villain. In fact, there's even a sticky weed that is named after him. It's called Sticky Willie – perhaps because Charlie had such trouble shaking off Cumberland's redcoats while he was escaping. And there's a similar weed called Stinking Willie, because Butcher Cumberland was a real stinker!

But Charlie will always be a fairytale prince, handsome and courageous, whose quest brought glory and honour to lots of people. Take the clan warriors of the Highlands. Thanks to Charlie's rebellion, people everywhere began to realise that Highlanders make tough, loyal soldiers.

And Charlie is still helping people. Thanks to him, tourists from all corners of the globe flock to the Highlands of Scotland to learn about his exciting adventures.

Let's face it, everyone has a soft spot for Bonnie Prince Charlie. There are loads of songs and poems about him, like 'The Skye Boat Song' and 'Charlie Is My Darling'. There's even a tasty recipe called Chicken Bonnie Prince Charlie!

And if you want to know what it feels like to be a real hero, all you have to do is find a kiltmaker and try on the Bonnie Prince Charlie Highland dress. Close your eyes and imagine the sound of pipes and drums, as a thousand Highlanders rush over a hillside ready to follow you on a great adventure. Where the adventure leads is up to you.